OUT OF THE WOODLAND

BY ALEXANDRA KETTLES

ILLUSTRATED BY
STEPHEN HOFFE

This book is dedicated to Eva G and Thomas (Mr Muscles) with whom I spent a glorious week

during the summer holidays.

Thank you for the laughter, loudness,

curiosities and caring acceptance.

Love to you both!

Author	Alexandra Kettles
Illustrator	Stephen Hoffe
Editor	Milena Wolmarans

ACKNOWLEDGEMENTS

Special thanks to Robert, Milena, Clara and Catherine for your support and encouragement. It will not be forgotten.

Contents

1
The Cotswolds

Charlotte and Thomas live in a six-bedroom, sand-coloured brick home in south central England. It is here where the rolling hills and woodlands hold secrets that few can hear or see or even…… feel!

Only the gifted have the privilege of knowing what lies within Cotswolds' gardens and beyond.

I would like to take you on a journey through this enchanted countryside and the lives of Charlotte, aged eleven, and her brother, Thomas, aged eight. Charlotte is about to begin High School and loves to ride her pony Crackers, while Thomas simply cannot live without his transformers, superheroes and Lego.

They have a black Labrador called Edward who always gets up to mischief; environmentalist parents, Clare and Oliver, and two friends, Danny and Eva, that they just met on their summer holidays.

This is Charlotte's story.

It all began in what everyone called the 'African summer' of 2018. Our gardens were arid, mum said, and restrictions were placed on watering – mine and Tom's school installed a dual flushing system in the toilets and our sports fields were not watered at all.

The school grounds, normally abuzz with bees and butterflies, seemed unusually quiet. As we drove home, the pyramidal orchids - well that's what dad calls them - wild geraniums, poppies, cowslip and daisies were hardly seen in the meadows or verges.

We had always been told how lucky we were to live in such a beautiful area. I do believe Thomas and I enjoyed the colours that showed the seasons, as well as the freedom the countryside gave us.

However, that summer, I remember the rolling hills had turned a shade of brown. We sweltered.

That is when things began to change.

It was coming up to the summer holidays. Mum had warned me that riding after nine thirty in the morning and before five in the afternoon was not allowed because Crackers, my palomino, would suffer in the heat. Dutifully after school I waited to ride and as soon as the day started to cool, I ran to the stables to tack up. We were going to hack the bridle path through the woodland - it circled the farmers' fields and crossed the river Windrush.

On this occasion Thomas had asked if he could join me on his mountain bike.

"Do you promise not to bother Crackers on the hack?"

"I promise," exclaimed Tom, with all the excitement of a late afternoon adventure. We put on our helmets, reported our route to mum and set off - Tom on his bike, me on Crackers and Edward following behind.

2
The first glimpse!

$\mathcal{B}$y the time we left the stables it was nearing six o'clock. The bridle path took us along the hedgerow of Mr Tarrant's grazing field, then to the bottom of a hill, which Tom whizzed down with Edward in hot pursuit. Crackers knew this route so well and so did I. Trotting, then slowing to a walk, we finally entered the shady woodland that grew beside the river. All four of us revelled in the coolness beneath the trees.

Tom rode ahead as Edward bounded to catch up.

"Charlotte look what I've found," he called.

"What is it?" I replied.

Edward was full of excitement and could hardly keep still; his body wriggled like a worm.

"Tom, what is it?" I repeated.

"I'm not sure but it's not what we normally find!" exclaimed Tom. He was holding his fishing net in his left hand and his right hand was pointing at something.

I needed to get closer. I couldn't see properly.

"What's that?" he asked me.

I really wanted to dismount but knew better, so I walked Crackers to the river edge and let him have a drink. Out of the corner of my eye I could see, or I thought I saw... uuum... errr... a big snake? A mouse? A baby otter? I don't know what I saw, but it left a wiggly trail!

"Tom! Tom!" I called urgently as he inched closer.

"Do you have the phone?"

I wanted him to take a picture. Tom ran back to his bike and ruffled through his bag to look for it.

"No, I must have left it at home," he pouted.

"Drat!" I muttered under my breath as Crackers spooked and backed into the river. I turned him in a circle, which quietened him down and no sooner had I accomplished this, a gentle whispered sound came out of the woods.

"Can you hear that Tom?" I whispered.

"Can you hear that?"

Crackers, Edward, Tom and I held our breath, staring wide-eyed towards the woodland. For a split second I wasn't sure if I was scared or not.

Suddenly, Tom moved. He jumped up from fright and tried to turn. One foot caught on the open bag strap at his feet and the other foot landed in the biggest patch of mud...

Tom skidded to a halt as his arms flew out to steady himself. He looked so stricken - I'm not sure he even realised he had landed in the river. Covered in mud, dripping wet, he ran to his bike, climbed on and headed home up the hill as fast as his legs could peddle him.
Edward was inches behind, barking all the way.

That was all it took. Crackers and I followed at a canter, arriving at the stables just as mum called us for dinner.

I untacked and settled Crackers for the night then ran to the house. I was just in time to catch Tom washing his hands in the bathroom.

"Don't tell anyone what we heard or saw Tom," I pleaded.

"Why not Charlotte? What was it?" questioned Tom.

"Just don't tell anyone. Not yet anyway – we must go back tomorrow after school."

"Okay, Charlotte, I won't tell a soul."

"Promise?"

"I promise," said Tom.

As we entered the dining room where mum and dad were already seated, mum was serving up dinner. We sat down calmly and, you wouldn't believe this but, no sooner had we sat down, Tom opened his mouth!

"Crackers spooked today, and Charlotte almost fell off!" Tom burst out.

"No, I did not Tom! You are lying," I said, kicking him under the table.

"*Charlotte!*" Dad rebuked me.

Tom and I sat up straight in our seats. I'd been caught... I rolled my eyes and sighed. Tom always gets away with things, it's just not fair!

Dad assigned me dishes as punishment. Tom smiled...

"Why did Crackers spook Charlotte?" asked mum continuing, "he knows the area so well and this is not like him."

Tom was about to answer but in desperation I replied rather loudly.

"Oh, he didn't really spook! He backed into the river, so I turned him, and he settled down. It must have been a bird or something silly like that."

Tom stared at me.

"Right," said mum, "you had better ride Crackers in the field tomorrow, perhaps for a day or two. Goodness," she went on, "this weather is getting to us all."

"Good idea mum and yes, the weather is sticky," I said as I scratched a bite on my leg.

A big smile spread across my face as I thought, *I'd done it - I had saved the day*. Nobody knew about the mystery woodland whispers.

Washing the dishes didn't seem so bad after all.

3
Shadows & Shivers

One week. It had been one week and nothing; no glimpses, no whispers or eerie feelings. Tom and I had gone to the woodland early morning and after school for the past week to look for signs of what we had seen that late afternoon. Not even a buurr, burrb or burble echoed from the trees. Or so I had thought. There was no sign that anything existed beyond our own imaginings.

Did it happen, I wondered?

One good thing came from returning to the woodland - Tom found the fishing net he had dropped in his mad dash for home.

The summer days were hot but glorious. Early morning rides in the fields were full of birdsong as the Robins, Thrushes, Wagtails and Warblers also began their busy day.

The long, lazy afternoons were always interrupted by the *bzzz* of mosquitoes and midges, especially down by the river. I didn't like them much as they always made me itch. The late suppers that overlooked the lawns made up for them though. It meant a lot of extra chores for Tom and me, but we didn't mind - Edward loved it!

It was a Wednesday in the middle of August when dad was home late. Tom and I stayed up longer than usual, going to bed just as night was falling, about half an hour after sunset. There was an eerie atmosphere at dusk. Mum had given Tom and I a break from chores and Tom had wandered to bed about fifteen minutes before. As I climbed the stairs on my way to my room, I heard him crying. I poked my head around his door to see what was wrong.

"Tom, are you okay?" I whispered.

"No," said Tom, sheepishly.

"What's wrong?" I asked.

"I think they are back," exclaimed Tom with nervous apprehension.

"Who's back, Tom?" I entered his room and closed the door.

"I'm not sure!" he replied, "but they are back!"

I sat on the side of his bed as Tom pointed to a shadow on the curtain.

"They're there," he said.

I turned to look where he was pointing. The light from outside had lit up the window and the curtains creating shadows that from deep within the realms of our minds looked like creatures from beyond – we both screamed!

Then they were gone!

Tom and I sat in stunned silence.

We heard dad coming up the stairs... the creaking of the wooden staircase becoming louder as he ascended.

We looked at each other and with a quick pinky-promise, before dad could open the door, I ran across the room and grabbed one of Tom's transformers. Dad popped his face around the door and asked, "Everything okay? We heard screaming."

"Oh, sorry dad, just playing transformers," we both piped up. He smiled and ushered me out of the room, saying good night to Tom as we left.

I lay in bed, for what seemed like hours, waiting for the house to be quiet. When all was calm, I slowly opened my door, stepped out and crept to Tom's room. The light under his door created a pattern on the landing carpet. Softly, I tapped with my knuckle then entered. Tom was playing with his Lego.

"Tom, how are you?" I could see by his facial expression that he had been scared.

"You told me not to tell anyone, but I've seen them, and they scare me Charlotte."

I suddenly felt very guilty. Poor Tom! He kept his promise, had been scared and didn't even tell.

Looking down I asked,

"Will you forgive me?"

"Of course," he said, without hesitation, as I ruffled through the drawing book I held.

"Look, I drew a picture of what I saw. Did you see it Tom?"

"Yes, I did! Perhaps not as clear as you, Charlotte, but I did see it!" Tom exclaimed.

Charlotte had drawn a slug-like creature, camouflaged within the shadows of the curtain. The moonlight outlined it, bringing the creature to life.

We shivered.

4
Scary Stuff

I woke late and missed my morning ride on Crackers; Edward was barking near the greenhouse and I could hear someone in the bathroom. *Drat.*

I swung my door open and right there in front of me was Tom.

"Morning," he said.

I felt proud of Tom; he had kept his promise, braved the unknown and was still standing - bravo Tom! I wanted to give him a reward of sorts, but what? I knew just the thing.

"Tom, would you like to go fishing today?" I asked him.

We hadn't been down to the river for a couple days after our last disappointing visits. This made me think of the creatures... then Tom answered.

"Charlotte, I would like that. When?"

"Let's get dressed and head down there now. I wonder if mum would make us a picnic." She did.

The heat persisted with very little chance of rain. Not being able to ride Crackers, I took my bike from the garage. Tom and I rode through the fields into the woodland until we reached the river. As we were about to unpack a voice called out.

 "Hello."

We looked up and saw a boy with the curliest black hair I had ever seen.

He wore blue jeans, a tatty t-shirt and a pair of shoes that had more holes in them than Tom's fishing net.

"Hello, who are you? What are you doing here?" I asked.

I felt protective of this area as we didn't see people here often. *Who is this person?* I wondered. I knew if dad was here, he would have put me right back in my place; after all, it was a public footpath.

"My name is Daniel; Danny my mum calls me. Dan to my friends."

"Hello, Dan. I'm Charlotte and this," – before I could finish Tom introduced himself…

"Thomas, I'm Tom. This is Edward," he stated, pointing to Eddie.

"Pleased t' meet you, Charlotte, Tom and Edward. I love dogs." He nodded politely before continuing, "We're here on holiday so I thought I'd wonder down these public paths - exploring you know."

He had a slightly different accent.

"Where are you from?" asked Tom.

"I've come up from Wiltshire! Born an' bred, that's what mum says."

"I don't think we've been to Wiltshire. Is it far?" Tom asked.

"Only an hour or so down the road. What are you doing?" he finished.

"We haven't been here for a while, so we thought to have a picnic and catch some fish," stated Tom, proudly holding up his fishing net.

"Please join us," Charlotte found herself saying.

Tom crouched near the river and Dan followed suit. I rolled my eyes - boy talk, I guessed. I lay out the picnic blanket, put the basket on top of it and went to join them as they fished.

When our tummies started rumbling, we sat on the blanket and ate our lunch. The birds fluttered about chirping in the cool breeze as the river trickled along over the stones.

They glistened in areas where the sun caught the water. It was so peaceful.

"WWAAAAAAAAAHHH!" yelled Tom, as he leapt up and flicked his arm up and down.

"What is it?", "Tom, what's wrong?" demanded Dan and I together as we jumped to his rescue.

"It's a spider," Tom barked, as he ran around shaking his arm.

"Oh, don't be scared, don't be scared. Stand still and let me help you!" laughed Dan, running around after Tom.

Things started to calm down after Dan grabbed the spider from Tom's arm and placed it on his hand.

"It's probably more scared of you than you are of it. Do you know that spiders are called Arachnids?" Danny's voice rose with enthusiasm, "They're short sighted an' make silk! They spin webs t' catch their food an' it can take a whole hour. They work quite hard".

Tom took a step closer to the spider and so did I!

"You should not fear them. Look, look at its

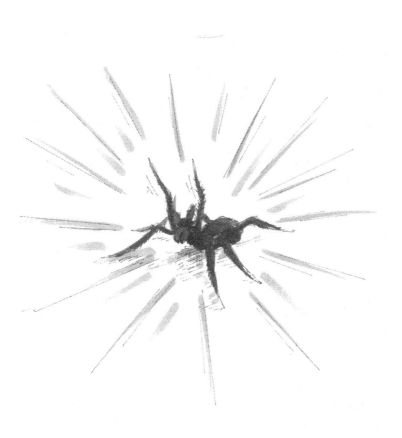

feet," Tom and I moved even closer - "do you see the hairs on his feet so he can hang upside down on ceilings?"

"Oh yes, how clever!"

I remembered dad telling us to not be scared but we never listened and ran away with mum following.

"We are almost always in the company of a spider," added Dan, "but they don't hurt you, do they?" he quipped. "It's only when you see them and fear them that mayhem starts. Here, try holding it."

I did but Tom, even though he didn't run away, only just managed to touch it!

"My dad always tells me to never fear – to fear less then fear not, especially when nature can be so kind. Mind you, I'm not sure about Africa an' their spiders!"

We all laughed…

..then Dan released the spider on the ground without a to-do.

5
Simple Silence!

Tom and I thought about what Daniel said about fear. It prompted us to decide that if we should see the slug-like creatures again, we would not fear them, and we would not scream. I guess that may be easier said than done!

We had planned to go to the river this morning then changed our minds. At first, we thought it would be fun to explore the riverbed for tadpoles, fish and insects. Then we remembered the drought. The river had gone from knee deep to ankle high, so we agreed to avoid the woodlands until the rains came.

We hoped to see Danny again but felt quite confident that he would knock on our door if he was in the area.

Rather than going down to the river, mum booked a riding lesson for Tom in the late afternoon. I decided to pamper Crackers and wash his mane and tail. The day passed without any major event – warmth, laughter and plenty of lemonade.

I watched Tom's lesson. Halfway through, I heard mum and dad arrive home from work. I decided to wait for Tom to finish so we could both walk Crackers to the stables. We turned him out after hosing him down and checked his stable. Crackers was making the most of it and rolled on the ground then rose to munch away at the grass.

We headed to the house.

Over dinner, our parents told us that Sunday we would have lunch at the Rat and Rabbit in the village. That was exciting news - their Sunday lunches were the best! Dad mentioned something about a visiting colleague and mum rambled on about Paige and an ornithology conference in Arusha, Tanzania. Whatever that was. I shrugged my shoulders and Tom followed suit.

It must have been about quarter past eight when the table was finally cleared. We could see the kitchen from the dining room. The top window was open. Mum could be seen by the sink, running the tap with her back to us while dad could be heard putting the plates away. That's when we saw it!

"Look, Tom, look!" I whispered. Tom turned to look at the open kitchen window. Silence fell… he didn't say a word.

We didn't scream, we didn't panic, we just... gawked.

As dusk fell, neither light nor dark, three of these creatures had begun to descend, awkwardly, from the window.

"Tom, they aren't slug-like at all. Look, Tom! They have feathers and fur." I couldn't have said it quieter. Turning to face the kitchen Tom nodded in agreement.

Mum must have caught sight of them from the corner of her eye – as she stacked the dishes with her left hand, her right hand grabbed the fly swotter and...

We didn't want to look. Tom and I both held our breath and squeezed our eyes tightly shut. We opened them one by one. Edward barked.

"Are they dead, Charlotte? Are they dead?" Tom's voice quivered.

"No, they made it – they are behind the curtain Tom, they made it!"

We had to act fast.

Tom grabbed the butter while I picked up the salt and pepper. We rushed to the kitchen to distract our parents.

"We'll finish the dishes," we said simultaneously.

"Well that's kind of you two," dad said.

He looked at mum and raised an eyebrow.

We couldn't wait for them to leave the kitchen.

"Wow Tom! Did you see them more clearly this time?"

"I did," Tom gasped, "they have big round eyes!"

"I know! And feathers, fur and tails."

We continued to watch the curtain but didn't see them again.

Tom and I went to bed happy that night. We were proud of ourselves for staying silent when we noticed them and for being so composed and unafraid. It gave us a sense of achievement. We knew then that the creatures weren't harmful at all and felt rather silly for our previous behaviour... screaming, indeed!

6
Cotswold Creatures

Holidays were ending. The days shortened, pony club slowed down and I didn't want the summer to end. The weather remained warm with little rain, but the drought held without a downpour. Tom and I took stock, making notes of everything we had seen and remembered about the creatures.

Sitting in the conservatory with paper, pen and coloured pencils ready, we started.

"I remember big marble eyes Charlotte! Bigger than Jane's at school."

"Yes! I saw those too. I think I even saw an eyebrow." I screwed up my face as I tried to remember.

"What, like ours?" Tom laughed as he continued, "Animals don't have eyebrows."

I giggled, "Well, Edward sort of does but maybe I'm wrong. They moved so fast! Let's draw some and pick the best eyes."

"What else do you remember?" Tom asked.

"Um, tails! I saw a tail," exclaimed Charlotte.

"What did it look like? I'm not sure I saw a tail."

"It was a bit like a duster - it curved and then fluffed at the end."

"Was it fur or feathers?"

"I can't remember" I admitted.

"Draw both Charlotte - you are so good at it. Please draw both," Tom begged. Excitedly, he added "I think I saw tiny wings."

"Wings? Are you sure Tom?"

"Yes, wings, I saw wings." Tom was quite confident now.

"Fur or feathers?"

"Feathers, definitely feathers!"

This was all quite fanciful and none of our descriptions seemed to make any sense.

This is what I drew.

I wondered if anyone else knew what they were.

Tom and I, drawing in hand, searched all of mum's reference books as we tried desperately to match the wings to the best of our ability. I even re-drew the wings at Tom's request.

It took the whole morning to gather our thoughts on the creatures. We took a break for lunch and then continued in the late afternoon with our notes.

"What else do we know?" asked Charlotte, "other than us always seeing them at dusk?" Charlotte added this as item one on her list.

"We know they were in the woodland. Mmm, aaand curtains - they liked the curtains."

"They don't like loud noises," Charlotte added, scribbling down more points. They sat thinking for a long time.

"They left a trail, Charlotte, by the water's edge. They left a trail. Remember?"

"They did, you're right Tom. Good thinking!"

Charlotte included it in their list and added an extra item at the end...

The List

1.   We see them at dusk

2.   They live in the woodland

3.   They hide in the curtains

4.   They don't like loud noises

5.   They leave a trail behind

6.   Maybe they're scared of humans

"I'm going to add a couple more points Tom and if we remember anything, we can add it later."

"Oh, yes and they have long bodies." Tom said.

He smiled feeling chuffed with himself.

Charlotte quickly added that to the list too.

7.   Long body

8.

9.

They closed Charlotte's drawing inside the notebook and placed them in the cupboard where no one else would see.

7
A Super Sunday Lunch!

"Come on everyone, I want to get there early." Dad was standing at the open front door. "Come on," he pleaded.

In a flurry we scrambled into the car and set off on the road to the Rat and Rabbit for our Sunday luncheon. We arrived early and I was surprised to see that we were seated at a table for twelve.

"Who's joining us Dad?" I questioned.

"The colleague I told you about last week." I suddenly felt shy. Luckily, they had not arrived yet.

"Can we go outside and play," Tom asked as he walked his transformer across the tablecloth.

"Off you go, we will call you once everyone has arrived."

"Thanks Dad."

Tom and I raced outside. Tom beelined for the jungle gym. I thought it rather small for me and chose a swing – I tried to reach the sky. Imagine our delight when I started to descend and saw Daniel.

"Dan," I hollered. He raised his arm to acknowledge us as he walked towards the play area.

"Hello." I greeted him.

"Hi Charlotte, how are you?"

"I'm good, thank you. What are you doing here?"

Tom was running towards us waving his transformer in the air as he approached.

"Hi Tom, good to see you – I think our parents know each other. They're all sitting inside."

"Really? Is your dad a colleague?"

"No, my mum." We all laughed.

Perhaps this was going to be a great afternoon after all.

No sooner had we finished catching up when a rather smaller looking young girl started to walk towards us with great confidence.

"Hello everyone," she said.

Her hair was thick and crossed between mousey brown and ginger'ish; she wore a French braid tied with a pretty lilac bow. She had sun kisses (freckles) all over her face and hazel eyes.

"Pleased to meet you." I said, "this is Tom, Daniel and I'm Charlotte."

"My name is Eva," replied the girl, smiling.

We hit it off from the beginning. Tom and Dan went back to the jungle gym while Eva and I chatted on the swings. She was from Jersey in the Channel Islands.

"I've never been to Jersey. Is it far?"

"We had to take an aeroplane, but not for long and then drove about an hour." Then she added, "It's pretty here, isn't it?"

I had to agree, we loved it. Without any further thought, Eva and I laughed and giggled as our swings went higher and higher. This was so much fun!

"Lunch," somebody called.

In our happiness we skipped, ran and chatted to the restaurant. Our parents rose from their chairs and introduced us. I hadn't realised Dan had an older brother named Luke.

He was fifteen, spotty and looked a bit scary;
he was on his cell phone... always!

Eva had a baby sister, called Katie, who was perched in a highchair between Eva's mum, Paige, and her dad, Josh; she was cute.

We all sat down and in no time at all were looking at the menu and ordering.

What a smashing meal! I had roast potatoes, carrots, peas, butternut, roast beef and the best Yorkshire pudding you can imagine. All smothered in gravy. Yum!

8
Thunder &
Lightning!

Monday morning – work and school. Quick breakfasts before grabbing our ties and searching for shoes and P.E. kits.

"Come on, come on, come on!" urged Dad.

We were out the door!

DooF! DooF! DooF! DooF! CLICK

The car rumbled to life and we were on our way. First Tom and I, then mum was dropped off. The week had begun.

It felt like the longest week of my life. I couldn't concentrate at all, no matter how hard I tried! I was told off by almost all my teachers. I jumbled up my words in English, couldn't subtract properly in Maths, didn't even take part in the Science quiz. Oh, and I was given extra star jumps to do in PE! All I could think about were these creatures. I wondered if Tom was struggling too. What a relief it was when the weekend finally came!

It was September. The winds had picked up and the promise of an imminent downpour was clear. It was darker than usual outside; clouds covered the sky.

Tom was in his room with the door open playing lego while I sat on my bed looking at my creature drawings and our list.

All was peaceful until Edward started to bark by the greenhouse outside. Tom decided to go and see what was wrong.

I watched from my bedroom window as he crossed the gravel driveway and made his way towards Edward.

Thunder and lightning - it was going to pour.

"Hurray here comes the rain," I announced, as I clapped my hands in excitement.

That's when I noticed Tom - he was waving his arms like crazy, trying to get my attention. Edward had dashed to the house, but Tom just stood in the rain.

"Charlotte! Charlotte, open the windows! *CHARLOTTE!*" shouted Tom, with urgency.

I opened my window immediately, running to Tom's room to do the same.

"Whatever is it Tom?"

"The creatures fear the rain!" he called back.

I could see Tom opening the greenhouse door and mayhem in the garden as the creatures took cover. They even dashed to the stables.

I ran down the stairs, out the door and straight to the stables to check on Crackers, but he seemed fine. Sitting on his bottom were not ONE, not TWO, not THREE but FOUR creatures!! I wondered if they had climbed his tail.

They looked wet, cold and frightened.

Tom ran towards the stables.

"Are they okay?" he puffed.

In that moment, we became fully aware of them. *What should we do?* I thought. Crackers was calm so we stood for what seemed ages, then flew into action.

"Get straw, umm, is there a basket? Do we have blankets? What do they eat? Should we get them some water?"

We had so many questions!

We scraped bits and bobs together and soon a cosy bed was made in the corner of the stable, propped up against a beam. It looked sort of like a nest. Surprisingly, one by one, the creatures floated across. I wished it wasn't so dark.

Before long, all was calm in the stables.

Then we remembered there were creatures in the greenhouse too! We raced there as fast as we could to make more nests, this time using peat in flowerpots.

Tom and I could not believe our eyes! There were a lot of creatures. We were so afraid of scaring them away that neither of us moved. At least that's what I thought until a movement

caught my eye. Keeping my head as still as I could, I glanced over at Tom. His eyes were almost as big as the creatures and he had the biggest grin on his face. His hands were clasped together under his chin and his legs bounced up and down on the spot. He was positively buzzing! I don't think there was one part of him that didn't move.

In his excitement, Tom looked my way. He must have seen how stiff I was standing because we both suddenly burst out laughing!

Then we noticed the creatures. They looked quite frightened at our outburst. Tom and I quietly left, returned to my room and watched from the window until we couldn't see outside anymore, which was no time at all.

9
Artwork

Everything looked fresh the next morning. The birds were singing, and it seemed the plants smiled too. Rain puddles were all over the place. Tom made a point to splash in them wherever possible.

After school, we completed our homework then went to my room to update our list and drawings.

"Let's start with the drawings Tom."

The eyes...

"Not so big! More round and marble-like."

I drew the eyes as Tom described.

"What about the tail, Tom? Did you see it this time?"

"I tried. It was difficult in the dark, but I think I saw one. It was feathers - fluffy feathers."

"Yes, I agree." Charlotte drew a feathered tail, which looked like her last attempt at it. "I'm going to add the body," Charlotte decided.

Tom peered over her shoulder.

The sketches looked almost perfect.

"What about our list?" he asked.

Tom and Charlotte added more points:

8.   They float or fly

9.   They're scared of water

10. ~~thr~~ They don't only live in the woodland

11. They try to hide everywhere

12. May not fear people

Charlotte added even more.

13.

14.

I began to sum up what I thought and decided to start a diary.

Dear diary   September 2018

My first sighting

I thought these creatures were slug-like, dark, and perhaps even nasty. The type of creatures best left alone in the imagination never to surface again .... how wrong I was!

They glide along the ground, but they weren't like slugs at all. They seem to float or fly as well?!?

I do know they become frightened like us and look for hideaways so they can't be hurt. They are very wary of things.

They seem to like being around other animals. Well, at least Crackers and Edward. Although Edward does bark a lot.

I ♥ animals too.

I can't help but wonder why they come out at dusk because it can be such a scary time of day. They seem to like it... or... perhaps they don't like the night. Sometimes I think it can be eerie too but once I settle then I sleep well. I wonder if the creatures do too?!

I do hope we see them again and find out more.

Charlotte Ford

Once again, after our sighting the creatures disappeared. Not much happened next. In fact, it seemed as if they had vanished. I started to think it had something to do with the rain when out of the blue they re-appeared!

It was dusk. Seated across from each other at the dining table, with opened textbooks, writing paper and pens, Tom and I were concentrating so hard on our homework that we almost missed the event! Luckily, a feather landed right in front of us.

A split second later, a creature fell from the ceiling and thumped on the table... and slid to the floor. Tom and I laughed.

Desperately, we tried to help but it quickly dodged us on the ground. It floated and moved with such ease that we simply couldn't keep up then poof! It was gone.

We had a feather! Tom and I stared at it.

It was so difficult to work out!

The creatures seemed to float but they couldn't remain in high places for long before they fell with a soft thud. They moved fast to avoid people or objects yet were clumsy and slipped and slid around. They had fur and feathers, which softened them, making them look friendly but I remember drawing them angry and irritable in our drawings at the start.

We were frightened in the early days. Now when we saw them, we wanted to help and protect them.

What were these creatures? I really wanted to know!

10
Everyone
Comes to Stay

"Hurraaay!" it was Sunday the 21st of October and the mid-term school break had begun. We were all expecting the arrival of Danny and Eva's family for four nights. I was so excited I didn't know what to do with myself.

Mum and Dad prepared extra goodies to eat and it seemed the house was abuzz with goings-on. Edward was bathed, Crackers' mane and tail groomed, and the lawn cut to a shorter than usual length.

I ran downstairs, skipped to the dining room and stopped in amazement. The table was laid with our best cutlery, crockery and glasses – there were flowers on the server and candles as a centre piece. Wow! It looked decorative.

"Charlotte," mum called.

"Coming," I replied.

I arrived and saw Tom standing between mum and dad as Edward sat patiently, ears perked, in front of them. Coming up the driveway was a blue car that I didn't recognise until I saw Eva's face appear in the back window.

There was so much excitement, it felt like a Christmas family get together. Tom and I showed Eva around the house and as we entered my room, we heard another car pulling up outside. We ran to the window and looked out to see Danny wave. Edward greeted him at the door as we ran down.

"Hello everyone," Tom, Eva and I said in unison. There were so many replies and greetings, I couldn't tell who was saying what.

"Eva are you okay to share a room with Charlotte?" mum asked her. We both nodded enthusiastically as she continued, "Luke, would you mind sharing with your brother?" Luke looked up from his tablet and nodded.

"Splendid! Then perhaps little Katie could sleep with her parents, Paige and Josh."

Mum had everything organised and directed the whereabouts of each guest to their upstairs room.

Eva and Danny unpacked their bags before the four of us headed to the garden and stables beyond. We showed them the whole property including Mr Tarrant's fields. We reached the house just before dusk.

Sunset was a lot earlier this time of year and there was a definite chill in the air. Eva and I decided to play a board game, so she ran next door to ask Tom and Danny if they wanted to join us. They did.

We could hear our parents' downstairs and the occasional disapproving whimper from Katie. The smell of dinner wafted through the air. The four of us sat on my bedroom floor as I dealt the money while the others chose their tokens. I was the horse.

Suddenly, Danny piped up, "Did you hear that?"

We all had. I pulled Tom to one side of the room and whispered,

"Tom should we tell them about the creatures?"

He seemed to think it was a great idea, so we did. I'm not sure they believed us. Nonetheless, we told them as much as we could remember and showed them our sketches and the list we made.

"There's the noise again," said Danny.

"Are you trying to scare us Charlotte?" questioned Eva.

"No, really it isn't me or…" before I finished, in the shadow of dusk, six creatures could be seen awkwardly clambering through the window. They hid behind the curtains.

We all stared in silence.

"Wha'? What? ... I can't... I don't... flip!" exclaimed Danny, as he sat up straight. Tom and I were so glad they hadn't screamed.

"Let's sit still for a minute or two. We don't want to scare them. Let's see what happens." I opened the list and drawings again and placed them on the floor in front of us. Eva hadn't said a word yet.

It was the first time the creatures showed themselves on purpose. They floated out from behind the cover of the curtains and landed in different places of the room – one or two with an ungainly thump. Speechless, we sat in silence.

What now? I thought. None of us knew what to do. We just sat and waited and watched without uttering a word.

Eva's arm shot out as she pointed across the room – her finger waggled up and down as she exclaimed in excitement.

"Aaaaw! Look how cute its face is!"

We all followed her gaze. I blinked in surprise.

"They do have eyebrows, Tom!"

You can't imagine what happened next! Danny's brother Luke burst through the door!

"DINNER!" he shouted.

We all jumped up in protest.

"That's not funny," grumbled Danny.

"Why did you do that?" Tom complained.

"Go away Luke!" Eva rebuked him.

My eyes quickly scanned the room, but the creatures had scattered. Once again, they were gone.

"I've been told to come and fetch you, so let's go," Luke said.

We followed Luke out the door and sulkily trudged down the stairs behind him, muttering our disapproval.

I couldn't believe he had scared them away!
I decided right then and there that he was
mean.

Then I heard Eva giggle softly behind me. I turned to see what she found so funny and saw that Tom was looking too. There, at the top of the landing was Danny. He was mimicking one of the creatures – one hand was tucked behind his bottom like a tail, and the other was on his forehead with two fingers poked up for eyebrows. He wiggled his body and we couldn't help but laugh.

Luke swung around.

"What are you all laughing at?"

We covered our mouths and tried to look serious as we shrugged our shoulders. No one was ready to talk to Luke yet.

Tom had stopped to wait for us at the bottom of the stairs. Silently, he raised two fingers and tapped them twice on the side of his arm – a secret sign for the creatures.

We all shared a smile as we copied him.

11
What to Call Them?

The excitement continued through dinner; the table laughter, how Katie fell asleep while we ate, our parents as they talked non-stop. Yes, it was a good evening. While the adults were distracted, we all arranged to meet in my room later that night.

Eva and I talked and talked while we waited. When the knock on our door finally came, I think we had both fallen asleep because we woke abruptly, jumped out of bed and hobbled to the door.

A short while later, the four of us sat in a circle on the floor. Tom and I filled Dan and Eva in on all the details we missed out before and tried to answer all the questions they had.

That's when Eva came up with an idea to name the creatures.

What fun it was!

"Skinks!"

 "What is a Skink? laughed Tom.

"What about **Gloops?**"

We all laughed this time while continuing to call out random names.

"Marbles Eyes is too long," said Charlotte

"Flufftails!" added Eva.

It didn't matter who said what, we just kept going with name after name after name until....

12
The Goobie Dash

I woke up late. I threw my duvet off, leapt out of bed and turned to look at Eva. It surprised me to see she wasn't there. I grabbed my dressing gown and ran downstairs to find everyone (except our parents and Katie) having cereal at the breakfast nook.

"Morning everyone."

"Morning Charlotte," echoed the threesome. Luke only nodded.

"What an evening. Goobies!" I said, for no apparent reason. It started a very interesting discussion; which Luke didn't even notice – he was still on his phone.

We made another list of what we wanted to know about the Goobies.

We made a pact - we were going to get some answers this bank holiday!

We finished breakfast and headed to our rooms to dress.

Danny burped on his way up the stairs.

"Gross Danny," scolded Eva as she turned to look at us. Tom looked at Danny and shrugged.

Eva and I ran to my room, closed the door, lay on the bed and giggled!

It was a cool day; not cold by any means but cool. Clouds filled the sky and there was hope of rain. We both put on our jeans and a t-shirt and headed out – we had Goobies to find!

Tom and Danny were already outside. We met them on our walk to the greenhouse; Edward followed.

"So where shall we search?" Tom asked.

"Let's look around the greenhouse. Edward often barks there, and we've never understood why. Perhaps he's always known about the Goobies."

I smiled - it sounded so much better to say

Goobies rather than creatures. We moved pots, looked behind bags of soil, under tables and garden chairs – nothing.

"Look what I've found," beamed Danny, proudly.

Tom, Eva and I raced to his side and peered at the greenhouse floor. There, on a red brick, lay a feather and two small tufts of fur.

"The Goobies have colour!" Tom exclaimed, showing us the green feathered tip.

"That wasn't on the last feather was it?"

"No, definitely not, Charlotte," Tom replied, confirming what I thought, "It feels different too! This one's a lot rougher."

"Look, look! There's fur!" Charlotte said in surprise as she rolled the small tuft between her fingers.

"It's not as soft as you would think."

We marched out of the greenhouse towards the stables and took the feather and fur with us. Crackers was happily dozing in his paddock, which left us free to inspect our treasure without any interruptions. Whilst there, we searched the stable, tack room and hay barn in the hope of finding more. It wasn't until we got to the food bins that we discovered another feather.

"It's smaller than the last one," Danny said as he gently picked it up.

"It's got a yellow tip," added Tom.

We all leaned in to get a closer look as Danny held the feather towards the light of the stable door.

"Ooooh nooo," Eva groaned, as she glanced past the feather, "Look!"

The clouds were swirling in the sky, they were menacing.

Danny pointed up, "I reckon it's going to pour down! We had better get back to the house."

The skies opened as we took our first steps out the door and what a sight we saw!

The garden had erupted into action and from every direction we could see Goobies racing for the greenhouse – and right towards us!

There must have been at least thirty of them that ducked and dived for cover; some moved along the ground and others floated about, but they all darted as quickly as possible towards the closest building.

Eva had to dodge numerous Goobies; Danny tried to catch one and Tom, brave Tom, stood his ground and watched them. He was delighted to see the carousal of commotion.

How could Tom and I forget they didn't like water? I slapped my forehead in frustration.

I felt like an idiot.

While everyone else ran around, watched for Goobies and tried to control Edward, I hurried to fetch Crackers, led him to the stable, rubbed him down and put up a hay net. By the time we eventually reached the house we were all drenched.

What excitement!

As you can imagine, our afternoon was filled with Goobiness!

13
The Attack

We didn't see the Goobies the next day at dusk - it must have been the rain that prevented them from coming in through our bedroom windows. We couldn't think of any other reason. The Goobies wouldn't be shy, after all we were passed introductions.

In a way, it gave us time to ponder.

The morning went rather quickly. Up early, we piled into cars and headed to a nearby town where an antique automobile show and a craft fete had attracted many visitors and tourists. Town was busy.

Luke had wondered off, much to the worry of his parents, Rachel and Kyle Butterworth. He re-appeared later for lunch. His parents hardly uttered a word to him the whole afternoon, but he didn't seem to mind.

In the late afternoon, we headed home.

As dad drove up the driveway, I noticed Edward barking aggressively near the greenhouse. Eva and I turned to look out the back window to signal Danny and Tom in the car behind. They saw us. Moments later, both parents pulled into the garages and we all hopped out the cars and ran to help Edward. Racing around the house at top speed, I fell.

"Charlotte are you okay?" shouted Eva.

I had grazed my knee and it was bleeding. "I'm alright, Eva, keep going," I urged, as she ran past me.

I got up and continued to run, finally catching up with the others.

"That looks sore," said a concerned Tom.

"Is it sore?" questioned Danny.

I wanted to reply but Edward's bark drew our attention. He was holding his own, surrounded by Goobies. We stepped in to help. Waving our arms above our heads we tried in vain to stop the Goobies from attacking Edward.

What was going on?

It took us some time to stop them. Eventually, as usual, they disappeared.

Well, at first that's what we thought, but had they really? …

We all looked more carefully and this time we saw them!

It was a

to the garden pots to hide.

A-HA! We knew where they had gone now. We turned our attention to Edward who, despite his ordeal, was wagging his tail and smiling – if dogs could smile. He looked proud of himself.

Once things had calmed down, I sat on the grass and tended to my knee. The blood had dried but I could see it was badly grazed.

"Let's go clean that up Charlotte."

"It really is fine Eva," I replied.

The boys rummaged around the pots as they tried to find the Goobies.

"I don't see any of them, Danny, do you?"

Reluctantly Danny had to agree.

"Not one Goobie to be found."

We thought we had them!

"What time is it?" asked Tom.

"Six-thirty," replied Eva.

It was dusk, and it was getting chilly.

There was an eerie atmosphere around the garden. Things had changed. The Goobies had attacked Edward. I muttered under my breathe.

"They attacked Edward."

"What does all this mean?" Tom sighed as he looked up at Eva.

"I don't know, Tom, I don't know."

I cleaned up my wound and put a plaster on it.

14
Crackers Kicks Out

There was so much to think about. The Goobies, the attack on Edward and everyone about to return home.

Eva helped me write my diary today.

Dear Diary   October 2018

A horrid event happened yesterday! Edward our Labrador was attacked by the Goobies. We had to rescue him. I fell over and grazed my knee.

There was a Goobie dash to the flowerpots to hide. We saw them but when Danny and Thomas went to find them, they had disappeared.

There are so many mysteries. ~~On top~~ On top of everything our visitors are leaving tomorrow. Sorry about the mess. Katie is sitting with Eva and I while I write.

Today will be a pleasant last day!

Charlotte Ford,

Eva Parsons & Katie

Everyone stayed in that morning. I guess they wanted to relax before they travelled. Danny and Tom set their sights on building a new fort, while Eva and I played. We lay on our tummies, legs in the air and chatted as we role played. We thoroughly enjoyed it. My room and Tom's looked like a creative jumble of toys – I'm not sure our parents would have seen it the same way.

Over lunch, Eva and I decided to go for one last ride. We wanted to use Mr Tarrant's field, as the sheep had been moved to the bottom one, near the woodland. It was arranged.

At three-thirty, we groomed and tacked up. I rode first through the wooden gate, which Eva closed behind us. As we walked the hedgerow and watched the rabbits, the last of the sun's rays warmed us.

"I love riding," I said to Eva as I dismounted.

Eva hesitated, "I've always been afraid of horses. Until now that is." She smiled and mounted. We continued our ride.

The ride was short but enjoyable. On our way back, Eva said,

"I shall miss you, Charlotte, and all the shenanigans. What do you think will happen to the Goobies?" She looked down at me.

"I don't know Eva. I will keep you updated." As we both agreed this was the best idea, we looked up and spotted Tom and Danny pushing their bicycles down the driveway.

"Hello, you two," called Tom as he smiled and waved.

"I was just agreeing to keep Eva and Danny updated on the Goobies" I told him, nodding towards Dan.

"Oh yes, please! That'd be really cool'. Let's exchange cell numbers?" Danny suggested.

"I'll have to ask Dad," said Tom.

Back at the yard we untacked and groomed Crackers, but just as Tom passed me the hay net, Crackers kicked out.

"Woah! Steady!" I soothed Crackers as I held the halter and stroked his neck.

"What has gotten into you?" I asked him.

"Over there!" exclaimed Tom as he shifted around Crackers to get a better look.

"No there!" – Danny jumped to the side and pointed.

"There, there, look!" Eva shouted from the stable door.

Scurrying through the straw and climbing up the stable walls were the Goobies!

"They must've startled him," Eva said.

"You're probably right. I'll take Crackers out."

I walked Crackers out into the stable yard while Thomas, Dan and Eva gently tried to shoo the Goobies away.

SHOO SHOO SHOO

Danny and Tom burst into laughter as Eva accidentally took a step back into a fresh pile of horse poo.

"Eeeeew," she said as she shook her foot about. "That's not funny!"

But she knew it was and soon joined the others in their laughter.

"Look, look, look!" called Charlotte from outside. "You did it! The Goobies are leaving." She turned Crackers and headed back to the stable.

No harm was done, but I still didn't understand what had happened. They hadn't affected Crackers in this way before. This was another worrying event.

We needed a meeting.

15
Let's Tell Someone

The four of us marched upstairs as Mr & Mrs Parsons reminded Eva not to sleep late. They had an early start in the morning and would be travelling by eight.

We headed into Tom's room.

"Right," I started, "Edward and Crackers have both been bothered or seemingly attacked by the Goobies," my voice was getting louder.

"Is this intentional? Are the Goobies *actually* mean?"

Thomas answered first.

"I think they could be afraid of Edward," he said as he shrugged his shoulders, "there seems to be more of them now. Maybe it's to defend themselves or maybe they're just

111

being mean."

"What do you think Danny? Could we be in danger too?" I continued, "Are the Goobies mean do you think?"

"I'm not sure either," Eva said. "We can't seem to catch them. First, we saw a few but now there are many! Is it strength in numbers or are they...?"

Danny interrupted her, "Let's tell someone older than us. They might have a different view of things."

"That's true, but whom?" asked Eva.

There was a long silence...

"Let's tell my brother!" Danny said.

We all gasped.

"Luke?" I said, aghast. "But he doesn't like us. He is mean to us!"

"He isn't really you know. He just plays games

all the time. He's withdrawn and involved in the cyber world."

"Cyber world? What's that?" asked Eva, looking at me.

"It's a virtual world of exoplanets and multi-universes. It's not real," Danny explained.

"Cool," added Tom with a smile, "I don't find him mean and I love the cyber world too!"

We sat in silence. It was broken by Tom.

"I'm in!" he exclaimed.

"Me too," said Eva.

"Okay, okay, let's tell Luke. Who's going to call him?" I asked.

We drew straws and I ended up with the short one. I pouted. Why me?

I walked down the stairs and looked over my shoulder at the three of them. I trudged downwards, skipping the last step, slunk into the lounge and slumped down on the sofa opposite Luke.

I was wandering how to start the conversation when he spoke,

"Every-thing okay over there, Charlotte?" he asked.

"Well, mm, yes, I guess. Well, really, um… we were, us four, um – could you come upstairs perhaps?" I stuttered.

It had all come out so wrong! I could feel my face turn red.

He raised an eyebrow, just like Dad.

"Okay, sure," he replied. I was quite surprised that he had spoken to me.

As we climbed the stairs, we looked up at the landing where Tom, Eva and Danny peered down at us from the bedroom door. Luke frowned as all three of them darted back into the room. I fidgeted nervously.

I waltzed in and sat on the floor, relieved to have some friendly backup. We all watched as Luke entered my room, hesitated, then sat on the floor and joined our circle.

"What's up?" he asked in a kind but disinterested manner.

"Do you promise to listen to us until the end?" Danny questioned.

"What's going on Daniel?"

"Promise first," Tom interrupted.

Luke sighed, looked down at his tablet and nonchalantly agreed,

"I promise."

We explained everything, from our first sightings to Edwards attack and Crackers kicking out. We showed Luke the drawings and our list. Then we sat... and waited...

The silence was broken by Luke, who threw back his head and erupted into a torrent of laughter just as a Goobie fell from the ceiling!

Luke sprung up from the floor, his pale face gave away his shock. He moved to confront the Goobie, but we managed to calm him.

"We've tried to catch them, but we can't. They are too quick," Danny said, shaking his head at his brother.

"What was that?" Luke gasped.

"We have told you already – it's a Goobie!" Eva rolled her eyes.

"Sit down Luke… pleease?" she begged. "We have a better chance of getting closer to them if we're calm and pretend to look busy."

Luke sat down, shook his head. We all sensed the Goobies around us.

"Are they robotic or mechanical?" – you could almost see Luke's mind ticking over as he considered the options. He was wide-eyed; they constantly darted from left to right.

"We don't quite know yet, but we've got feathers with yellow and green tips," I offered.

"And fur," added Tom, enthusiastically.

"I noticed the Goobies' eyes were very round. Do you think they're cameras?"

We answered Luke the best way we knew how.

Luke continued, "But it's impossible to have fur and feathers. Impossible!"

"Gosh, Luke, we simply don't have the answers. That's why we've told you in the first place. Do you think they could be aliens or something?" I asked.

"That would be awesome!" Tom and Danny revelled in the thought.

"Did Edward or Crackers have any bite marks or cuts or anything to suggest they were attacked?" asked Luke inquisitively.

We all looked at one another. We hadn't checked. Like a flash, Danny jumped up and ran downstairs to check Edward.

Luke didn't seem mean to me anymore – far more human. He hadn't picked up his phone or tablet for at least half an hour. He was, I'd say, rather pleasant and yes, maybe clever too.

"Not a mark on him," burst out Danny who panted from his race back up the stairs.

"Right, so no bites. Hmm… I've got to sleep on this!"

"But we all leave tomorrow," sighed Eva.

"Best to make a group chat then so we can keep each other posted on events," Luke said with such enthusiasm it made us all grin. He was going to help!

"We were supposed to have created one already but forgot." I added.

We entered the lounge as a group…

"Mum? Dad? Can we create a group chat together on our phones, please?" Tom and I asked.

After some negotiation and more than a few promises from us all, we were given permission. Luke, Eva and I were the members of the group.

16
Saying Goodbye

We had hardly slept a wink that night, but Eva and I were still the first to rise. We wanted this bank holiday to last longer. We didn't want to say goodbye.

After breakfast, everyone helped to pack the cars.

The Parsons were the first to leave with vows to keep in touch and an invitation to visit Jersey. Eva, Tom, Danny, Luke and I signalled our loyalty to the Goobies before Eva opened the car door, climbed in and closed it again behind her. I waved so hard I thought my hand would drop off!

The Butterworths remained for another hour, which gave Luke, Danny, Tom and I an opportunity to make plans. Luke was going to search the internet for any valuable information, while I promised to gather more facts about the Goobies. We'd keep in touch… definitely!

We had also come up with a plan for Tom and me to train Edward not to bark at the Goobies so we would know for sure that they weren't scared of him. We thought it wise to somehow train Crackers too, so he wouldn't kick them.

When they finally left, their car pulled out the gate and Tom and I ran alongside it, waving. We closed the gate and slowly walked back to the house.

This was the best bank holiday we had ever had!

Now we had work to do. Edward and Crackers had to be trained; we had to plan.

Monday was school.

Dear Diary   1 November 2018

The house is so quiet without friends here. I learnt so much this holiday. Mainly not to judge too quickly — I guess I understand the ~~exprestion~~ expression 'don't judge a book by its cover' now. After all Luke is a kind person and perhaps the Goobies are not so kind.

Tom and I have a ~~task~~ in training Edward and Crackers.

Everything feels unsettled though. There are whispers from mum and dad about visiting Jersey but it's not certain. Just like everything else.

Back to school tomorrow. High School — it's a whole new world. My second term.

Charlotte Ford & Edward

17
Window Wonders

I must have stood at my bedroom window a thousand times and not caught a glimpse of a Goobie. Tom and I always left them open for as long as we possibly could, but the weather took a turn for the worst and it became icy cold. Rumours spread that we were in for a big freeze.

Tom and I worried and wondered if the Goobies were okay. What had happened to them? We never stopped checking the stables and greenhouse and flowerpots outside, but we found absolutely nothing. Our weekly reports to the others seemed mundane.

We thought that maybe this was a good time to start to train Edward and let the others know how it was progressing. We decided to split the training. Tom would teach Edward and I would coach Crackers.

It seemed so difficult with Crackers though because no matter how often I irritated him with soft toys around his hooves, he never kicked out! Then I had a fantastic idea. Chickens!! I was going to ask Dad for chickens; three maybe four. Tom and I would have to put our heads together to pull this off.

We eventually came up with the idea to approach the subject from a monetary perspective. That night after dinner, when Tom had finished Edward's training, we sat in the lounge together with mum and dad, trying to pluck up our courage.

"Go on, Charlotte," said Tom, as he elbowed me in the ribs.

"Stop it Tom," I hissed.

Dad looked our way.

I took a deep breath.

"Dad?"

"Yes Charlotte," he answered, kindly.

"When we go shopping, we buy free range eggs and they're the most expensive, aren't they?"

"I believe they are Charlotte."

Mum looked my way as Tom started talking.

"My friend has chickens at home. They live on a farm and he says he collects fresh eggs from them every day."

"I'd love to do that! Would it be cheaper do you think?'' I questioned.

"It would be," dad agreed. He continued, "but who would look after the chickens? They must be shut up every night, fed twice a day, their eggs would need to be collected… the list of responsibilities went on."

"We could each take it in turns and have a timetable on the fridge," Charlotte suggested. "Oh, please dad? They would help us train Edward and Crackers too."

"I don't mind helping at all," beamed Tom.

"Actually, come to think of it, I don't mind either." Mum looked up and smiled.

"Mmmm, excuse me," Dad got up and went to the bathroom and the subject of chickens wasn't mentioned again for some time. I knew though – mum had sealed the deal. I just didn't know when it would happen.

Time passed. We trained, we struggled, and we reported it all to the group. Then, one Friday afternoon towards the end of winter, Dad came home with a trailer. I couldn't quite make out what was on it; it looked like wood.

"Charlotte, come quick! Dad's bought a chicken coop."

We rushed outside to help! We carried wood to the workshop with screws and wire and sheets of mesh... oh, it was so exciting! We were going to make our own coop!

"Tomorrow we assemble it," Dad said.

I didn't want to stop but I could see he was tired, and tomorrow was Saturday.

"But what about the chickens?" Tom asked. "Where will they sleep tonight?"

"The chickens will be safe in the shed overnight," he said.

It was the last task we had to do. Tom and I carried the big box to the shed. It had holes in the top and we could hear the chickens through it. They clucked in alarm as the box wobbled in our arms – we tried our best to keep it steady as we stepped into the shed and placed it on the floor in the corner.

"You promise you won't peek, Charlotte?" Tom begged before he ran off to find some chicken feed and water.

When Tom returned, we closed the shed door so the chickens couldn't escape.

We opened the box lid.

"Bantams!!" Tom exclaimed with a big grin, "and browns!"

I smiled too. They had the funniest feathered feet and I couldn't help but think maybe the Goobies would like them too!

Edward's barking woke us early the next morning. It reminded me that training was beginning today.

"Charlotte, get up!" Tom called, "The chickens are awake."

"I'm coming, I'm coming!"

By midday, the coop was built, and the chickens were inside.

Tom and I both continued training. By the second week, Edward knew the command to stop barking and he responded to all of us.

Crackers and I were doing well too. When the chickens roamed outside, I ushered them into the stable and around his hooves. He fidgeted at first and moved a lot. One day, Crackers kicked out so hard at a chicken that it flew through the stable door and landed on the cement in the yard.

It lay there for a few seconds, then got up and
scurried along as if nothing had happened – I
probably shouldn't have laughed but it was
so funny! Just like Edward, after a week or
two of training, Crackers was used to the
company.

We were ready for the Goobies; if we ever saw them again.

We told Danny and Eva about the dizzy chicken. They also laughed.

Once Edward and Crackers were trained, we had nothing much to report. Luke, Eva and I kept chatting but by the start of Spring our phones were quiet. No Goobies. No excitement. Nothing. I began to wonder if it wasn't all a dream.

I decided it was time to speak to Mrs Hall, my biology teacher. I hadn't plucked up the courage before, but this term I had gained more confidence and I found Mrs Hall quite pleasant to chat to. Maybe she would know why the Goobies had disappeared. There just had to be a reason! It couldn't possibly end here.

18
Common Sense

I prepared several questions for Mrs Hall and put a lot of thought into it. The next time I passed her in the corridor I arranged to meet with her on Thursday after school.

Tom had football practice, so the timing was perfect. I had a good hour to get to grips with a more scientific approach to finding out who and what the Goobies really were. It was a bit tricky without letting the cat out the bag.

"Good afternoon Charlotte."

"Good afternoon, Mrs Hall," I greeted her politely.

I took a deep breath then began...

"Last summer, my brother and I discovered a creature near the river. It became quite friendly, though we couldn't catch it or touch it."

"Go on," she encouraged.

"Well, no sooner had it appeared, it would disappear again.

Any loud noise frightened it away. We haven't seen it all winter."

"There is an easy answer to the last query Charlotte. I guess your creature hibernates like bats, bears or hedgehogs. Perhaps it has migrated for the winter. Lots of animals do that too. You could check the library for a book on it," she smiled.

I felt like an absolute idiot. Here I was in high school and I hadn't even given these a second thought.

"Can an animal have fur and feathers?" I blurted.

"No," Mrs Hall said gently, "fur is a mammalian trait and feathers we know belong to birds." She indicated toward the posters at the other end of the laboratory.

I glanced across the room. There was a table that showed the classification of all living organisms. Underneath the Kingdom Animalia were two distinctly different groups: vertebrates and invertebrates. I looked closely at the vertebrates - they were split into five more groups, *Classes*, Mrs Hall called them. Pictures of birds were under the title Aves and furry creatures were scattered around Mammalia.

Gosh! I didn't know how I would remember all these names. I cringed. Mrs Hall must've seen because she asked me if I wanted to take a photo with my phone. What a nice teacher!

"What about the creature disappearing?" I asked. "They do it so quickly and we can't find them, ever." I tried to make notes while Mrs Hall answered.

"A lot of animals move so fast you can't catch or hardly see them; some hide for survival too. You know," she leaned in to whisper, her eyes showing secrets while her mouth moved to a half smile. "Humans are scared of a lot of animals, but we are like giants to most of them."

"Perhaps the creature is like a chameleon and changed colour to camouflage itself. You may think it has disappeared but really it has blended in with everything around it."

Before I could say more, the homework bell sounded in the corridor. I packed my things into my school bag, thanked Mrs Hall and went to fetch Tom with a spring in my step.

Dad was fifteen minutes late. It didn't matter as after school activities meant the school grounds were still quite busy.

I filled Tom in on my discussion with Mrs Hall. By the time I finished we had both started to shiver. Dad arrived just on time – gosh it was cold. *Hurry up Spring*, I thought as I pushed a protesting Tom into the car.

"Stop it Charlotte," he moaned.

The trip home was quiet. Tom read a book, Dad muttered at everyone's driving and I was deep in thought about what I would write in my diary.

I had a photo to add to our collection of notes now; perhaps I could add in my own chart too. I wasn't certain if I would share this new information with the group.

Not yet, anyway.

The chart took a whole week to finish;
bearing in mind I had school and Crackers to
keep fit, as well as chickens to care for and
piano lessons. When it was done, I sent the
chart to Eva and Luke via our group chat.

GOOBIES

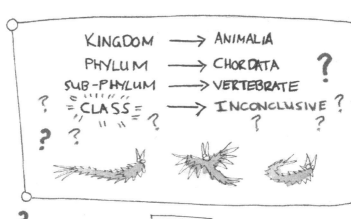

KINGDOM ⟶ ANIMALIA

PHYLUM ⟶ CHORDATA ?

SUB-PHYLUM ⟶ VERTEBRATE

? CLASS ⟶ INCONCLUSIVE ?
? ? ? ? ?

? ?

NOTES

- Not sure what they eat
- Possibly — hybernate
            — migrate
            — camouflage
- Not sure about breeding
- Not sure what they drink

Dear Diary   11 April 2019

I am quite sad that I haven't seen a Goobie since last summer. Perhaps we will never see them again.

It has been very difficult to classify them scientifically. They don't fit any of the descriptions I've seen. Luke now believes he didn't see the Goobies at all, which is awful!

Danny has taken over the group chat but because of the distance there has been a lag in communication.

I only really talk to Eva now. She is delighted with the chart. It all points to a Goobie being mythical – I wish we could see them again. Perhaps Luke is right.

Charlotte Ford (alone)

As Spring approached, bluebells and daffodils covered the landscape. Tom and I started to leave our windows open again. How we hoped to see the Goobies.

19
A Visit to Jersey

Suitcases packed, I tossed my rucksack over my shoulder and hollered for Tom to hurry up. Dad pulled the car up while mum rushed around the house and left notes for Sarah, our house sitter. We were going to Jersey.

Tom and I climbed into the back of the car, buckled up and smiled at each other as we high-fived... POW!

That was quite sore, but we were too excited to care.

The journey took at least an hour before we turned off to Bristol airport. Dad parked the car and unloaded the cases while mum marched to the ticket machine and returned with a trolley.

"Come on you two," said Dad.

"Coming," we responded as we raced to catch up.

"Look, look, Charlotte!" Tom pointed at an aeroplane that was about to land. "I hope I can find a plane transformer," he added with a wistful look on his face.

"Hurry up Charlotte, Tom, or we will miss our flight." Dad sounded tense.

We entered the terminal together and almost two hours later, we boarded the plane.

Tom sat by the window and I sat in an aisle seat next to him. Mum and Dad were directly behind us.

"Can I put your bag up Tom?"

"Yes, please Charlotte thank you."

We settled down for the take-off and chatted excitedly without a pause.

"We're taking off Charlotte, wow!"

We looked out the small window next to Tom.
I leaned in as best I could. Faster and faster we
felt the plane move; it rattled a bit and made a
funny noise before it lifted into the sky.

"Would you like a drink?" asked a steward once we were in the air.

"I'd like a juice please."

"Me too," Tom butted in.

"Crisps or croissant?"

"Crisps!"

"Croissant!"

We both answered at the same time. It made us laugh.

Once the steward moved on, I asked Tom if he would like his rucksack. He did.

I sat back down and began to munch on my snack as I unzipped my bag. I reached inside for a game and turned to ask Tom which one he would like to play, but before he could answer I yanked my hand out the bag with a little squeal.

"Tom, there are Goobies in my rucksack!" I whispered.

Hanging our heads over the rucksack, we peered in.

Two big pairs of eyes peered back at us.

Tom and I looked at each other.

"What do we do now?" he asked.

"We can't let them escape on a plane Tom, we just can't! There are so many people here – they'll probably get scared. We will have to keep them occupied."

"But how?" Tom looked genuinely worried.

"I know, let's feed them. What have you got Tom?"

He ruffled through his bag…

"I have a croissant, a strawberry lollipop, raisins and a chocolate. What about you?"

"I've got crisps, an apple and a little bag of sweets."

We fed the Goobies one treat at a time, but they didn't seem to like anything.

We were almost out of options.

"Wait! I've got pony cubes in the side of my rucksack, Tom. Should we try them?"

"Do it!" he said, as he tried to keep the Goobies from escaping.

I popped one into the bag. We waited for a count of two then peeked inside.

"Tom, look, they're eating it! That would explain us finding a feather near the food bins at the stables," said Charlotte as she fed each Goobie another cube.

"They love them!"

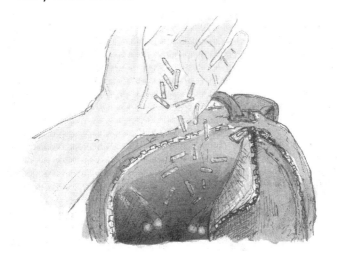

Tom leaned in to get a closer look but as his shoulder brushed the rucksack, both Goobies leapt from the bag and headed down the aisle.

An announcement from the captain requested everyone to return to their seat for landing.

"What should we do?" I whispered, and before I could even stop him, Tom unbuckled his seatbelt, stood up, grabbed some pony cubes and ran down the aisle to try to catch the Goobies.

The steward blocked him and sternly told him to go back to his seat.

It was too late!

As he turned, Tom tripped over his left foot and landed on the aisle floor directly on top of the Goobies!

Mum and Dad stood up to find out what was going on.

Tom was in double trouble!

Charlotte gasped.

"Tom you okay?" she called down the aisle.

An embarrassed Tom stood up, faced the steward and said,

"So sorry. I'm sorry, it was an accident."

He hung his head and turned to walk back to his seat. When he did look up, mum and dad's disapproving stare silenced him. This time Tom didn't mind; behind his silence was happiness as he could feel something wriggling in his pockets.

"Sit down," I ushered Tom to the window seat.

"What happened to the Goobies?"

"I think they are in my pockets Charlotte."

"How are we going to put them back?"

We fumbled with the rucksack and the pockets.

"Ouch," erupted Tom.

"Sit still," I urged him. "Use the pony cubes."

"Charlotte, Thomas, sit still and be quiet!" Dad said sternly.

"Put your pocket in the rucksack and empty them into the bag, Tom."

"What if they bite me?"

"They won't, Tom, do it!"

Tom squirmed and fidgeted.

"Done it! And they didn't bite."

I zipped the bag shut, sat back and sighed.

"It's never been that close, has it?"

"No, it has not!" Tom agreed with conviction.

The plane landed.

We were in Jersey! And we had somehow brought the Goobies with us.

I couldn't wait to tell Eva!

It's not over yet……..

'Beyond the Woodland'

Jersey, Channel Islands

Bursting to tell Eva what has happened Charlotte and Thomas arrive in Jersey with butterflies in their tummies – how could they possibly have a holiday with the Goobies!

Once Eva is told about the Goobies, and the secret is out the bag, the adventure begins. No part of the island is left untouched. These mythical creatures, the Goobies, come alive.

This fun packed sometimes seat gripping read takes Charlotte, Thomas and Eva to the Jersey zoo, the beach and on an island hunt exposing several environmental issues of today.

visit www.goobieadventures.com for more information.

Printed in Great Britain
by Amazon

71810369R00102